SCIENCE EVERYWHERE!

What Things Are Made Of

The Best Start in Science

By Helen Orme

New
Forest
Press

North American edition copyright © TickTock Entertainment Ltd. 2010

First published in North America in 2010 by New Forest Press,
PO Box 784, Mankato, MN 56002
www.newforestpress.com

TickTock project editor: Rob Cave
TickTock project designer: Trudi Webb

ISBN 978-1-84898-298-7
Library of Congress Control Number: 2010925593
Tracking number: nfp0002
Printed in the USA
9 8 7 6 5 4 3 2 1

Picture credits (t=top, b=bottom, c=center, l=left, r=right,
OFC=outside front cover, OBC=outside back cover):

Corbis: 13tl, 13bl, 14 all. Photodisc: 6t, 9t, 18t. Powerstock: 10b, 15tr.
Shutterstock: OFC all, 1 all, 2, 3 all, 4–5 all, 6c, 6b, 7 all, 8 all, 9c,
9b, 10t, 10c, 11 all, 12 all, 13r, 13cl, 14–15, 15t, 15b (both), 16 all,
17 all, 18b, 19 all, 20 all, 21 all, 22–23 all, 24t, OBC both.

Contents

Any words appearing in the text in bold, **like this**,
are explained in the Glossary.

Look at all the things around you. Have you ever wondered what they are made of?

Metal

Cotton plant

Trees

Look at the pictures of the
soda cans, the boys' colorful
T-shirts, and the books.

Now look at the pictures
of the **metal**, cotton plant,
and trees.

Can you match these things
with the **material** they are made from?

What are materials?

All the things around us are made from materials. We use different materials to make different objects.

Metal, **plastic, cloth, glass, paper,** and **wood** are some of the materials that we use every day.

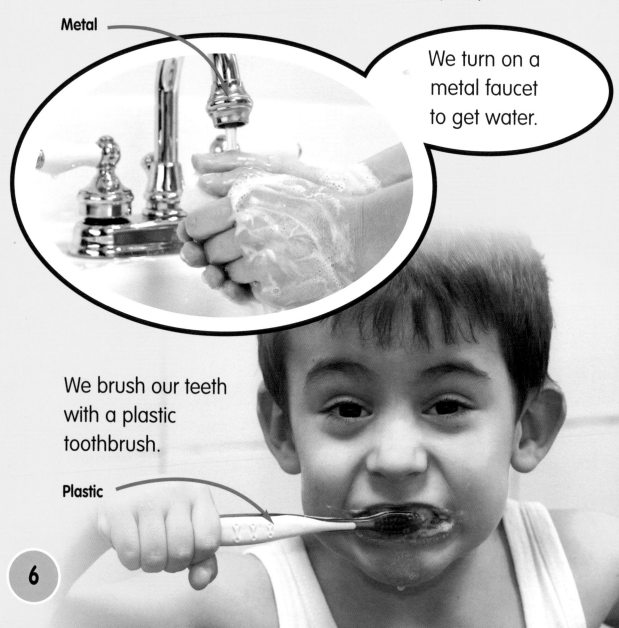

Metal

We turn on a metal faucet to get water.

We brush our teeth with a plastic toothbrush.

Plastic

Our clothes are made from cloth—come on, get dressed!

Cloth

Grownups like to read the newspaper.

Paper

We drink orange juice from a glass.

Wood

Glass

Open the front door—it's time for school!

Where does stone come from?

Stone is a hard, heavy **natural** material.
Mountains and cliffs are made of stone.

Mountains

Stone is dug out of the ground and from the sides of cliffs and mountains using diggers.

Digger

Stone does not bend, but it can be broken into pieces.

Rough stones

Smooth stones

Stone can be cut into shapes.

These huge stone faces have been cut into the side of a mountain in the United States.

Stone pyramid—4,500 years old

Many buildings are made from stone.

Stone lasts a long time.

Stone castle—600 years old

What is metal?

Metal is a material made from some types of stone.

Stone that contains metal is called ore.

Ore is smashed into powder. Then the powder is heated so that the metal comes out of the stone.

Iron ore

Copper ore

Metals are hard like stone, but they will bend.

Metal is a good material for making things like flexible fence wire.

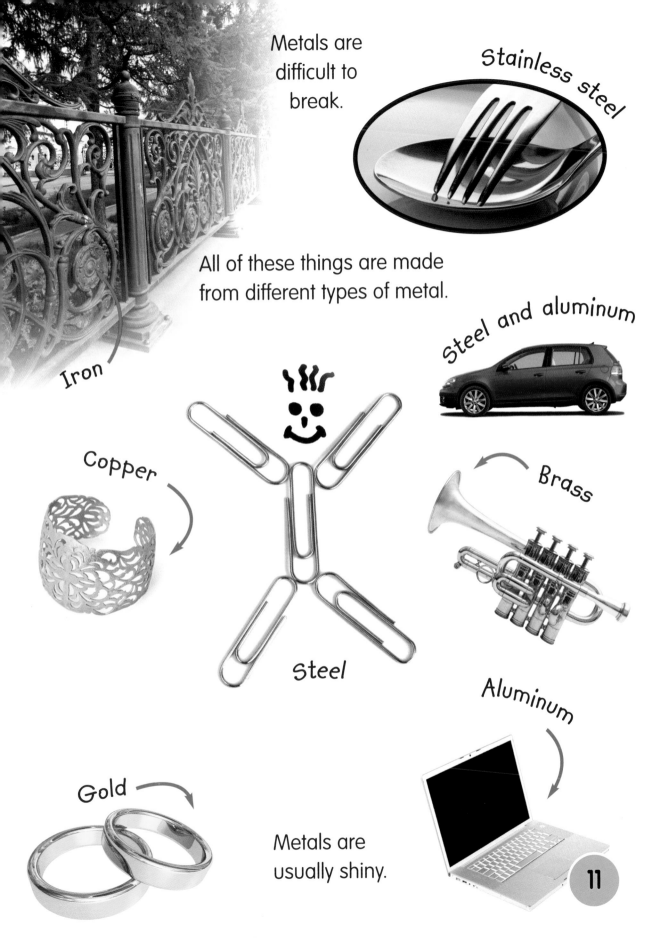

Metals are difficult to break.

Stainless steel

All of these things are made from different types of metal.

Iron

Steel and aluminum

Copper

Brass

Steel

Aluminum

Gold

Metals are usually shiny.

11

Where does wood come from?

Wood is a natural material. It comes from trees.

Wood

Trees

The trees are cut down using a chain saw.

Chain saw

The wood is taken to a factory called a sawmill.

The wood is cut and shaped with metal tools.

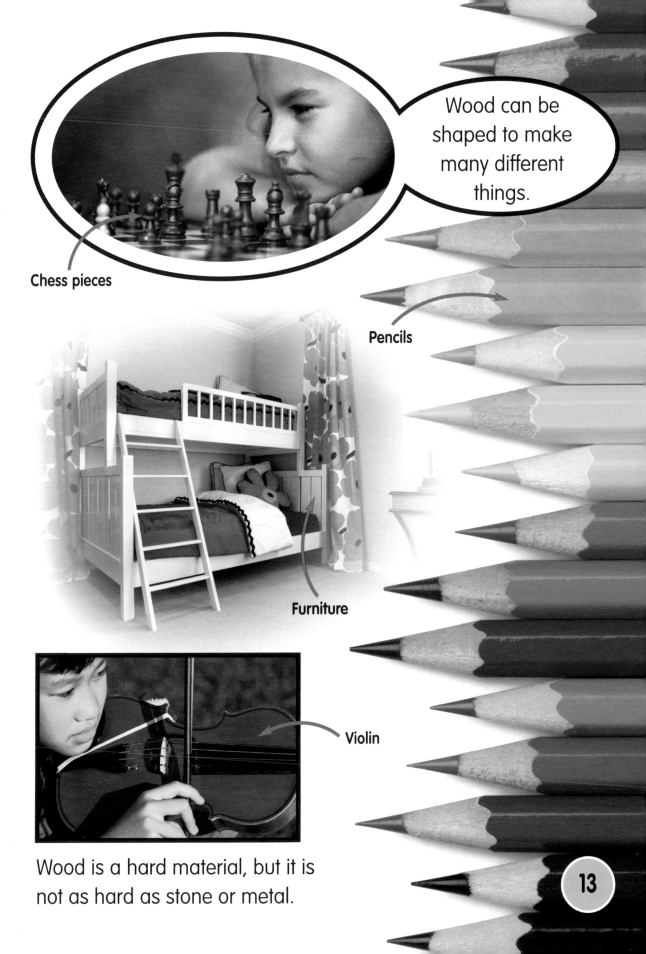

Chess pieces

Wood can be shaped to make many different things.

Pencils

Furniture

Violin

Wood is a hard material, but it is not as hard as stone or metal.

What is paper made from?

Paper is a soft **artificial** material that is made from wood.

Pulp

The wood is chopped up into tiny pieces. Then it is soaked in water to make a mushy mixture called **pulp**.

The pulp is then squeezed out into thin sheets and dried.

You cannot fold or bend wood, but you can bend and fold paper.

You can sit on a chair made from wood . . .

. . . but a paper chair would not be very strong!

Books

We use paper in many different ways!

Notebook

Wrapping paper

15

How is glass made?

Glass is a hard artificial material.
It is made from sand.

The sand is heated
until it is very, very hot.

The sand melts and
turns into glass.

Hot, soft glass

Hot glass is soft. It can be made into different shapes before it cools down and becomes hard.

Glass is **transparent**. This means that light can pass through it.

Glass windows let light in and allow us to see out.

We can see what's inside a glass container.

Clear glass bowl

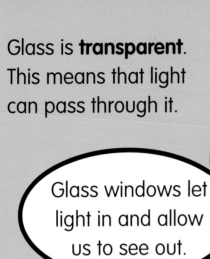

Don't touch broken glass!

The edges of broken glass will cut you.

17

What is plastic made from?

Plastic is an artificial material. It is made from **crude oil**. We find oil under the ground.

This machine is pumping oil from under the ground.

The oil is sent to a **refinery**.

At the refinery, the oil is heated to produce plastic and other useful substances such as gasoline.

Refinery

Plastic can be made in any shape and color.

Plastic can be bendable . . .

. . . or hard

. . . or soft.

Plastic bottle

Plastic bag

Plastic can also be transparent—you can see through it!

What is cloth made from?

Cloth is an artificial material made from **fibers**.

Natural fibers

Plastic fibers

Some cloth is made from plastic fibers. Some cloth is made from natural fibers.

Woolen cloth is made of natural fibers from sheep.

Cotton cloth is made of natural fibers from cotton plants.

The fibers are spun into a continuous **yarn**.

Then the yarn is made into cloth.

Cloth is a very soft material.

It can easily be folded.

Cloth is made into many things such as T-shirts, jeans, and sweaters.

Questions and answers

Q What is the pattern in wood called?

A It is called the "grain."

Q Look around your bedroom. How many things can you find made from metal, wood, paper, plastic, and cloth?

A Here are some ideas to get you started:
Pajamas—cloth
Books—paper
Sneakers—plastic

Q What can we do with used paper?

A We can recycle it! Used paper can be turned back into pulp and made into new paper.

Q Which animals can we get wool from?

A We can get wool from sheep, goats, alpaca, and llamas.

Alpaca

Q How can you find out the age of a tree?

A A tree grows a new ring inside its trunk each year. You can find out the age of the tree by counting the rings.

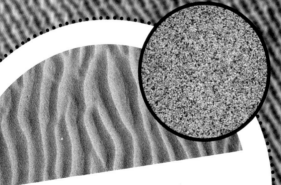

Q What is sand made of?

A Sand is made of millions of tiny pieces of stone.

Q What two materials is this hammer made of?

A Metal and wood.

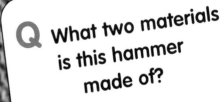

Glossary

Artificial Describes anything that is made by people.

Cloth A type of material that is made from fibers that have been joined together by weaving or knitting.

Crude oil Oil that has been pumped from under the ground. It is natural and has not had anything done to it by people.

Fibers Long, thin pieces of plastic, cotton, or wool.

Glass A transparent material made from sand.

Material Any substance that things are made from.

Metal A hard, strong material such as gold or steel.

Natural Describes anything that is made by nature.

Paper A lightweight material made from wood.

Plastic An artificial material made from crude oil. It can be formed into almost anything!

Pulp A mixture that is wet and mushy.

Refinery A large factory where crude oil is taken to be made into things such as gasoline and plastic.

Stone A hard, heavy natural material that can be dug from cliffs or mountains and used to make buildings.

Transparent See-through.

Wood A natural material that comes from trees.

Yarn A long thread made from fibers that have been twisted together.

Index